Ten Men

Complex
Words

Book 1

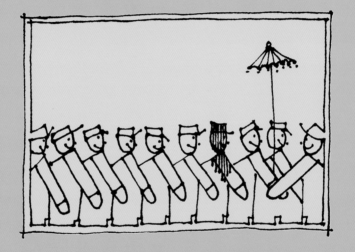

SCHOLASTIC

BOB
BOOKS

Ten Men

by Bobby Lynn Maslen
pictures by John R. Maslen

Scholastic Inc.

New York • Toronto • London • Auckland • Sydney • Mexico City • New Delhi • Hong Kong • Buenos Aires

Copyright © 1987 by Bobby Lynn Maslen. All rights reserved. Published by Scholastic Inc. *Publishers since 1920*. Published by arrangement with Bob Books® Publications LLC. SCHOLASTIC and associated logos are trademarks and/or registered trademarks of Scholastic Inc. BOB BOOKS are trademarks and/or registered trademarks of Bob Books® Publications LLC.

Lexile® is a registered trademark of MetaMetrics Inc.

35 34 33 32 31 30 29   20 21 22 23 24

Printed in China 68
This edition first printing, October 2020

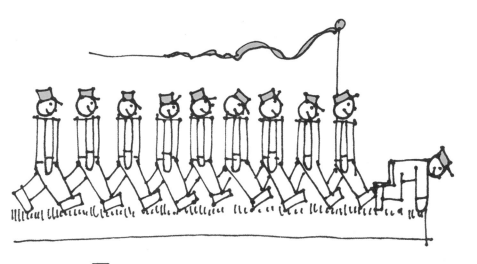

Ten men went to
the end of the land.

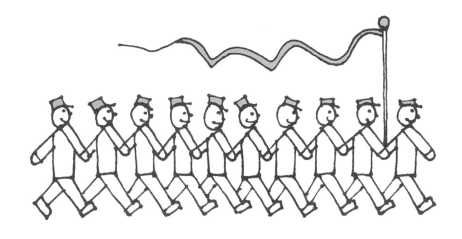

Hand in hand they went.

They went in wind.

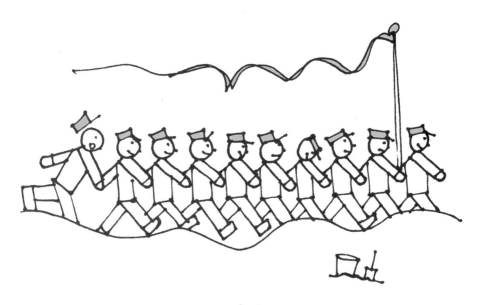

They went in sand.

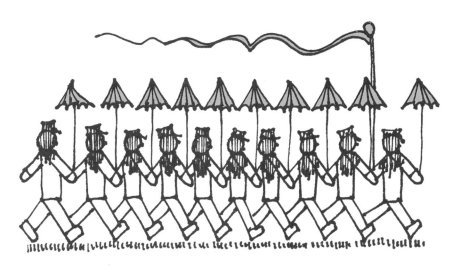

They went in sun.

Tim had a flag.

Jim had a drum.

Tim went fast.

Jim went last.

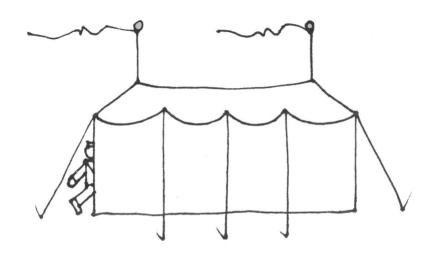

Into a tent the
ten men went.

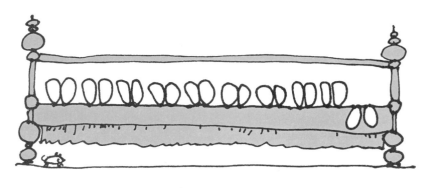

Then to bed the
ten were sent.

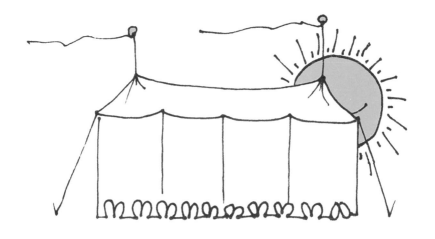

The sun has set on
the ten and the tent.

The End

Book 1 contains:

Short Vowels:

E	e	as in	elephant
A	a	as in	apple
I	i	as in	inchworm
U	u	as in	umbrella

Blends:

nt	-	tent		fl	-	flag
nd	-	land		dr	-	drum
st	-	fast				

The Complete Bob Books® Series

READING READINESS

MY FIRST
BOB BOOKS®
PRE-READING
SKILLS

MY FIRST
BOB BOOKS®
ALPHABET

STAGE 1: STARTING TO READ

SET 1
BEGINNING
READERS

FIRST
STORIES

RHYMING
WORDS

STAGE 2: EMERGING READER

ADVANCING
BEGINNERS

SIGHT WORDS
KINDERGARTEN

ANIMAL
STORIES

SIGHT WORDS
FIRST GRADE

STAGE 3: DEVELOPING READER

WORD
FAMILIES

COMPLEX
WORDS

LONG
VOWELS

Bob Books Apps
are available for
phones & tablets

www.BobBooks.com

Lexile® Measure: 60L
Guided Reading Level: E
Scholastic Reading Level: 1
Word Count: 64

Scholastic Inc.
978-0-439-17573

Bump!

Complex Words

Book 2

Bump!

by Bobby Lynn Maslen
pictures by John R. Maslen

Scholastic Inc.
New York • Toronto • London • Auckland • Sydney • Mexico City • New Delhi • Hong Kong • Buenos Aires

Copyright © 1987 by Bobby Lynn Maslen. All rights reserved. Published by Scholastic Inc. *Publishers since 1920*. Published by arrangement with Bob Books® Publications LLC. SCHOLASTIC and associated logos are trademarks and/or registered trademarks of Scholastic Inc. BOB BOOKS are trademarks and/or registered trademarks of Bob Books® Publications LLC.

Lexile® is a registered trademark of MetaMetrics Inc.

35 34 33 32 31 30 29   20 21 22 23 24

Printed in China 68
This edition first printing, October 2020

Sunny jumped.

Jimmy jumped.

Thumper jumped.

Skipper jumped and skipped.

Skipper and Thumper bumped!

Sunny and Thumper jumped up

Jimmy and Skipper jumped over.

Thumper skipped.

Skipper slipped.

Flip!

Jimmy and Skipper skipped.

Sunny and Thumper jumped up and over.

The End

Book 2 adds:

Blends:

mp	-	jump
sk	-	skip
th	-	thump
sl	-	slip

Endings:

y

er

ed

The Complete Bob Books® Series

READING READINESS

MY FIRST BOB BOOKS® PRE-READING SKILLS

MY FIRST BOB BOOKS® ALPHABET

STAGE 1: STARTING TO READ

SET 1 BEGINNING READERS

FIRST STORIES

RHYMING WORDS

STAGE 2: EMERGING READER

ADVANCING BEGINNERS

SIGHT WORDS KINDERGARTEN

ANIMAL STORIES

SIGHT WORDS FIRST GRADE

STAGE 3: DEVELOPING READER

WORD FAMILIES

COMPLEX WORDS

LONG VOWELS

Lexile® Measure: 80L
Guided Reading Level: F
Scholastic Reading Level: 1
Word Count: 40

 Bob Books Apps are available for phones & tablets

www.BobBooks.com

Scholastic Inc.
978-0-439-17574-

Cat and Mouse

Cat and Mouse

by Bobby Lynn Maslen
pictures by John R. Maslen

Scholastic Inc.

New York • Toronto • London • Auckland • Sydney • Mexico City • New Delhi • Hong Kong • Buenos Aires

Copyright © 1987 by Bobby Lynn Maslen. All rights reserved. Published by Scholastic Inc. *Publishers since 1920*. Published by arrangement with Bob Books® Publications LLC. SCHOLASTIC and associated logos are trademarks and/or registered trademarks of Scholastic Inc. BOB BOOKS are trademarks and/or registered trademarks of Bob Books® Publications LLC.

Lexile® is a registered trademark of MetaMetrics Inc.

35 34 33 32 31 30 29   20 21 22 23 24

Printed in China 68
This edition first printing, October 2020

Tilly is a kitty cat.

The cat can sit. The cat can skip.

She can nip. She can snap.

A mouse is in his house.

illy sat by the mouse house.

The mouse ran out of his house

The cat went slam, slap, snap!

The mouse ran fast.

"Help! Help! Stop that cat!"

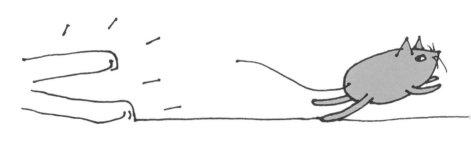

The mouse ran faster.

Tilly ran too fast.
Tilly went flip flop.

The mouse is happy to
be back in his house.

The End

Book 3 adds:

Short Vowel:
O   o   as in   octopus

Blends:

sn	-	snap
th	-	that
st	-	stop
lp	-	help
ck	-	back

Vowel Combination:

ou	-	mouse

The Complete Bob Books® Series

READING READINESS

MY FIRST
BOB BOOKS®
PRE-READING
SKILLS

MY FIRST
BOB BOOKS®
ALPHABET

STAGE 1: STARTING TO READ

SET 1
BEGINNING
READERS

FIRST
STORIES

RHYMING
WORDS

STAGE 2: EMERGING READER

ADVANCING
BEGINNERS

SIGHT WORDS
KINDERGARTEN

ANIMAL
STORIES

SIGHT WORDS
FIRST GRADE

STAGE 3: DEVELOPING READER

WORD
FAMILIES

COMPLEX
WORDS

LONG
VOWELS

Bob Books Apps
are available for
phones & tablets

www.BobBooks.com

Lexile® Measure: 60L
Guided Reading Level: F
Scholastic Reading Level: 1
Word Count: 75

Scholastic Inc
978-0-439-1757

The Swimmers

Complex Words
Book 4

The Swimmers

by Bobby Lynn Maslen
pictures by John R. Maslen

Scholastic Inc.

New York • Toronto • London • Auckland • Sydney • Mexico City • New Delhi • Hong Kong • Buenos Aires

35 34 33 32 31 30 29   20 21 22 23 24

Printed in China 68
This edition first printing, October 2020

It was summer. Pop, Stan, and Jim went to the pond.

Jim wanted to swim.
Stan wanted to swim.

Jim slipped into the pond.
Stan jumped into the pond.

Jim and Stan swam to a log.

"Step on the log, Jim," called Stan.
Jim slipped. "Jump on the log, Stan,"
called Jim. Stan slid.

"Stop! Stop!" called Pop.
The log spun.

"Help, Pop," called Jim.
"Help us stop, Pop," called Stan.

Pop wanted to help Jim and Stan.
Pop jumped onto the log, but
the log was a trap.

Into the pond went Pop.
Pop got wet.

Pop, Stan, and Jim got out
of the pond.

"Sit in the sun, Jim. Sit in a warm spot, Stan," said Pop. "Sit in the warm sun, Pop," called Stan and Jim.

The three swimmers went to
a sunny spot. The wet swimmers
sat happily on a warm spot
in the sun.

The End

Book 4 adds:

Blends:

sw	-	swim
sp	-	spun
tr	-	trap
rm	-	warm

Long Vowel:

ee	-	three

The Complete Bob Books® Series

READING READINESS

MY FIRST BOB BOOKS® PRE-READING SKILLS

MY FIRST BOB BOOKS® ALPHABET

STAGE 1: STARTING TO READ

SET 1 BEGINNING READERS

FIRST STORIES

RHYMING WORDS

STAGE 2: EMERGING READER

ADVANCING BEGINNERS

SIGHT WORDS KINDERGARTEN

ANIMAL STORIES

SIGHT WORDS FIRST GRADE

STAGE 3: DEVELOPING READER

WORD FAMILIES

COMPLEX WORDS

LONG VOWELS

Bob Books Apps are available for phones & tablets

www.BobBooks.com

Lexile® Measure: 310L
Guided Reading Level: G
Scholastic Reading Level: 1
Word Count: 149

Scholastic Inc
978-0-439-1757

Samantha

Complex Words

Book 5

Samantha

by Bobby Lynn Maslen
pictures by John R. Maslen

Scholastic Inc.
New York • Toronto • London • Auckland • Sydney • Mexico City • New Delhi • Hong Kong • Buenos Aires

35 34 33 32 31 30 29   20 21 22 23 24

Printed in China 68
This edition first printing, October 2020

The sun set.

Samantha went to bed.

"Good night, Sam,"
said Papa.

"Sleep tight, Samantha,"
said Mama.

The sun came up.

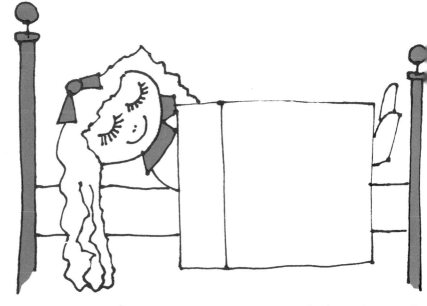

Samantha was still in bed.

"Get up," said Papa. Samantha
did not.

"Get up," said Mama. Still, Samantha did not sit up.

"Woof! Woof!"
said Roofus, the pup,
but Samantha did not get up.

"Tweet, tweet,"
said Sweetums, the parakeet.
Samantha was still in bed.

Mama cooked eggs.

Papa cooked ham.

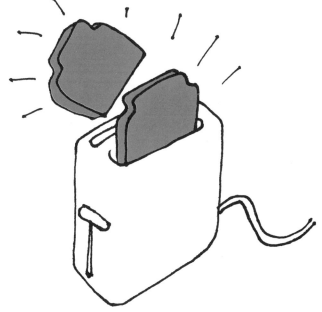

oast popped from the toaster.

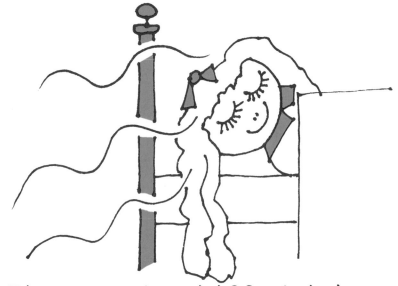

The smells whiffed into
Samantha's room.

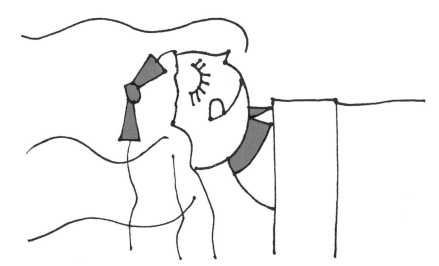

Her nose sniffed and sniffed.
She licked her lips.

Her eyes popped open.

Samantha jumped out of bed!

"Good morning, Mama and Papa," she said. "Good morning, Samantha," they called.

Woof! Woof!" barked
Roofus. "Tweet, tweet,"
sang Sweetums.

"Good morning", said the
bright sunlight.

The End

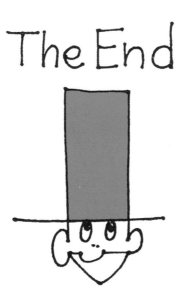

Book 5 adds:

Blends:

sm	-	smell	rn	-	morning
wh	-	whiff	ck	-	lick
rk	-	bark	ght	-	night

Long Vowel:
oa - toast

Vowel Combinations:
oo - good
ai - said

The Complete Bob Books® Series

READING READINESS

MY FIRST BOB BOOKS® PRE-READING SKILLS

MY FIRST BOB BOOKS® ALPHABET

STAGE 1: STARTING TO READ

SET 1 BEGINNING READERS

FIRST STORIES

RHYMING WORDS

STAGE 2: EMERGING READER

ADVANCING BEGINNERS

SIGHT WORDS KINDERGARTEN

ANIMAL STORIES

SIGHT WORDS FIRST GRADE

STAGE 3: DEVELOPING READER

WORD FAMILIES

COMPLEX WORDS

LONG VOWELS

Lexile® Measure: 210L
Guided Reading Level: G
Scholastic Reading Level: 1
Word Count: 127

Bob Books Apps are available for phones & tablets

www.BobBooks.com

Scholastic Inc.
978-0-439-1757

Willy's Wish

Willy's Wish

by Bobby Lynn Maslen
pictures by John R. Maslen

Scholastic Inc.
New York • Toronto • London • Auckland • Sydney • Mexico City • New Delhi • Hong Kong • Buenos Aires

Copyright © 1987 by Bobby Lynn Maslen. All rights reserved. Published by Scholastic Inc.
Publishers since 1920. Published by arrangement with Bob Books® Publications LLC.
SCHOLASTIC and associated logos are trademarks and/or registered trademarks of
Scholastic Inc. BOB BOOKS are trademarks and/or registered trademarks of Bob Books®
Publications LLC.

Lexile® is a registered trademark of MetaMetrics Inc.

35 34 33 32 31 30 29   20 21 22 23 24

Printed in China 68
This edition first printing, October 2020

Mama, Papa, and Willy went to a wishing well.

Willy threw three pennies into the wishing well.

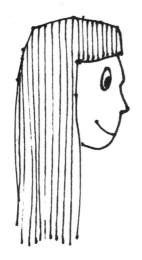

"What do you wish?"
      his mama said.

"What do you want?"
his papa said.

Willy put his hand to his head.
"I cannot think," is all he said.

His mama wished
for a red silk dress.

His papa wished for a baseball cap.

Willy put his hand to his head.
"I cannot think," is all he said.

Willy sat and sat. He put his
chin on his hand. "I have a
car. I have a cat."

"I have a ball and bat."

"I have a card game.
I have a jet plane.
What can I wish?"

Poor Willy sat and sat until the sun was almost set.

At last Willy put his hand on his tummy.

A wish came into his head, but he felt a little silly. He wiggled his nose.

He licked his lips.

He sniffed and sniffed.

The wish grew stronger and
stronger and stronger.

His mama looked.

His papa looked.

At last
Willy said, "I wish, I wish," as he
licked his lips, "for a big, big dish
of FISH and CHIPS!"

The End

Book 6 adds:

Blends:

wh	-	what	lk	-	silk
ch	-	chin	rd	-	card
sh	-	wish	lt	-	felt

Silent e:

a - e   baseball

o - e   nose

Vowel Combination:

ea -   head

The Complete Bob Books® Series

READING READINESS

MY FIRST BOB BOOKS® PRE-READING SKILLS

MY FIRST BOB BOOKS® ALPHABET

STAGE 1: STARTING TO READ

SET 1 BEGINNING READERS

FIRST STORIES

RHYMING WORDS

STAGE 2: EMERGING READER

ADVANCING BEGINNERS

SIGHT WORDS KINDERGARTEN

ANIMAL STORIES

SIGHT WORDS FIRST GRADE

STAGE 3: DEVELOPING READER

WORD FAMILIES

COMPLEX WORDS

LONG VOWELS

Lexile® Measure: 320L
Guided Reading Level: G
Scholastic Reading Level: 1
Word Count: 193

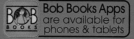

Bob Books Apps
are available for
phones & tablets

www.BobBooks.com

Scholastic Inc
978-0-439-1757

Jumper and the Clown

Jumper and the Clown

by Bobby Lynn Maslen
pictures by John R. Maslen

Scholastic Inc.
New York • Toronto • London • Auckland • Sydney • Mexico City • New Delhi • Hong Kong • Buenos Aires

Copyright © 1987 by Bobby Lynn Maslen. All rights reserved. Published by Scholastic Inc.
Publishers since 1920. Published by arrangement with Bob Books® Publications LLC.
SCHOLASTIC and associated logos are trademarks and/or registered trademarks of
Scholastic Inc. BOB BOOKS are trademarks and/or registered trademarks of Bob Books®
Publications LLC.

Lexile® is a registered trademark of MetaMetrics Inc.

35 34 33 32 31 30 29   20 21 22 23 24

Printed in China 68
This edition first printing, October 2020

A clown came to town!

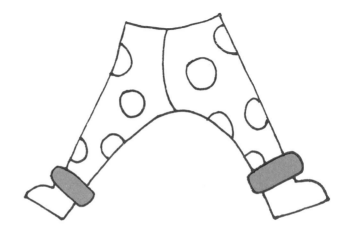

The clown had red pants
with pink dots.

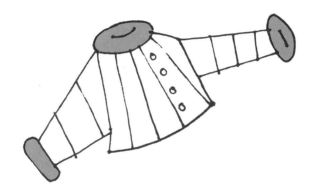

Her top was green and yellow.

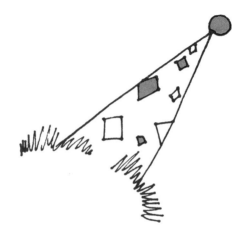

Her hat had spots of blue and orange.

She had
a round red nose and a
big grin. Her hair was purple.

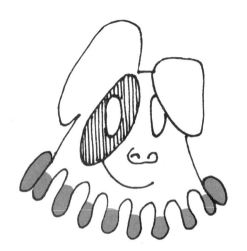

With the clown was a little
brown and black pup.

The pup was called Jumper.

"Up! Up! Jumper,"
          called the clown.

"Down. Jump down, Jumper,"
called the clown.

"Up! Down! Over! Under!"
called the clown.

Jumper jumped to the top.
Then he jumped down.

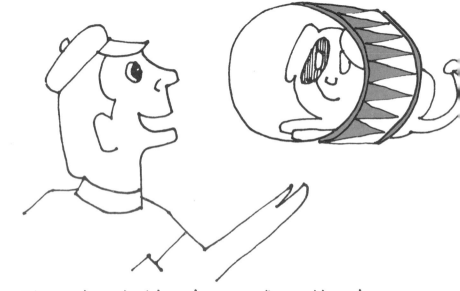

"Look at that pup," called a man
"Look at that clown."

"Let me see! Let me see!"
called all of the town kids.

Jumper jumped.
He jumped up. He jumped down.

The kids clapped their hands for the pup.

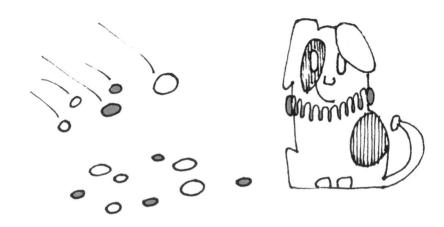

Then they tossed pennies
to the pup.

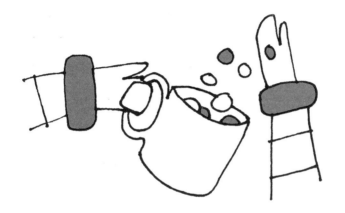

The clown put the pennies
into a cup.

The clown grinned a big grin.
She gave the pup a happy pat

hen the clown put a little gold
rown on the jumping pup.

As the kids clapped and cheered
the clown and the pup went on the
way to play in another town on
another day.

The End

Book 7 adds:

Blends:

cl	-	clown
gr	-	grin
wn	-	down

Colors:

green	red	blue
pink	orange	purple
yellow	brown	black
gold		

The Complete Bob Books® Series

READING READINESS

MY FIRST
BOB BOOKS®
PRE-READING
SKILLS

MY FIRST
BOB BOOKS®
ALPHABET

STAGE 1: STARTING TO READ

SET 1
BEGINNING
READERS

FIRST
STORIES

RHYMING
WORDS

STAGE 2: EMERGING READER

ADVANCING
BEGINNERS

SIGHT WORDS
KINDERGARTEN

ANIMAL
STORIES

SIGHT WORDS
FIRST GRADE

STAGE 3: DEVELOPING READER

WORD
FAMILIES

COMPLEX
WORDS

LONG
VOWELS

Bob Books Apps
are available for
phones & tablets

www.BobBooks.com

Lexile® Measure: 350L
Guided Reading Level: F
Scholastic Reading Level: 1
Word Count: 187

Scholastic Inc
978-0-439-1752

Max and the Tom Cats

📖 SCHOLASTIC

Max and the Tom Cats

by Bobby Lynn Maslen
pictures by John R. Maslen

Scholastic Inc.
New York • Toronto • London • Auckland • Sydney • Mexico City • New Delhi • Hong Kong • Buenos Aires

35 34 33 32 31 30 29   20 21 22 23 24

Printed in China 68
This edition first printing, October 2020

Six tom cats sit on the tiptop
of a big wall.

The sun will set soon.

"E-ow, e-ow, e-ow,"
all of the cats call.
"Me-ow, me-ow, me-ow," they squall.

Max, who is six, sits up in a tree.

"Hey, cats," calls Max, "what do you see?".

But the cats' "Me-ow" is all they will tell.

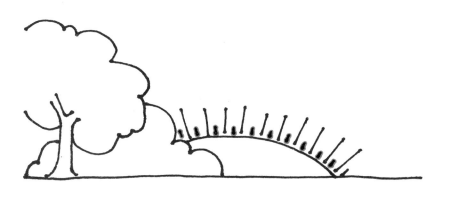

After a time
the sun did set.

As night fell, the cats called,
"Max, we see a big white ball."

Max looked up at the light as he sat in the tree. "What a wonderful sight," said he.

Then, as Max sat looking at the big white moon, he suddenly saw a man looking back at him.

The man in the moon saw six
cats and Max. "What a wonderful
sight tonight," said he.

Soon the bright light of the moon sat over them all.

Then the six tom cats did
begin to call and call and call.

"Me-ow, re-ow, bre-ow,"
they sang to Max
and to the man in the moon.

Max was glad
he was in the tree to see the
moonlight and to hear the song.

But at last the moon man
went out of sight. The song
was over until another night.

Go to bed, Max.

Go to bed, six tom cats.

Goodnight, Max.
Goodnight, Cats.

Goodnight, Moonlight.

The End

Book 8 adds:

x	-	six
sq	-	squall

Silent e:
i - e   white

The Complete Bob Books® Series

READING READINESS

MY FIRST
BOB BOOKS®
PRE-READING
SKILLS

MY FIRST
BOB BOOKS®
ALPHABET

STAGE 1: STARTING TO READ

SET 1
BEGINNING
READERS

FIRST
STORIES

RHYMING
WORDS

STAGE 2: EMERGING READER

ADVANCING
BEGINNERS

SIGHT WORDS
KINDERGARTEN

ANIMAL
STORIES

SIGHT WORDS
FIRST GRADE

STAGE 3: DEVELOPING READER

WORD
FAMILIES

COMPLEX
WORDS

LONG
VOWELS

Lexile® Measure: 490L
Guided Reading Level: G
Scholastic Reading Level: 1
Word Count: 217

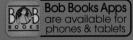

Bob Books Apps
are available for
phones & tablets

www.BobBooks.com

Scholastic Inc
978-0-439-1758